MW00910073

A Note to Parents and Caregivers:

Read-it! Readers are for children who are just starting on the amazing road to reading. These beautiful books support both the acquisition of reading skills and the love of books.

The PURPLE LEVEL presents basic topics and objects using high frequency words and simple language patterns.

The RED LEVEL presents familiar topics using common words and repeating sentence patterns.

The BLUE LEVEL presents new ideas using a larger vocabulary and varied sentence structure.

The YELLOW LEVEL presents more challenging ideas, a broad vocabulary, and wide variety in sentence structure.

The GREEN LEVEL presents more complex ideas, an extended vocabulary range, and expanded language structures.

The ORANGE LEVEL presents a wide range of ideas and concepts using challenging vocabulary and complex language structures.

When sharing a book with your child, read in short stretches, pausing often to talk about the pictures. Have your child turn the pages and point to the pictures and familiar words. And be sure to reread favorite stories or parts of stories.

There is no right or wrong way to share books with children. Find time to read with your child, and pass on the legacy of literacy.

Adria F. Klein, Ph.D.
Professor Emeritus
California State University
San Bernardino, California

For Rénu and Emilie, far, far away in Aveyron ...

Editor: Christianne Jones
Page Production: Tracy Davies
Creative Director: Keith Griffin
Editorial Director: Carol Jones
Managing Editor: Catherine Neitge

First American edition published in 2006 by
Picture Window Books
5115 Excelsior Boulevard
Suite 232
Minneapolis, MN 55416
877-845-8392
www.picturewindowbooks.com

First published in Canada in 2000 by
Les éditions Héritage inc.
300 Arran Street, Saint Lambert
Quebec, Canada J4R 1K5

Printed in the United States of America.

Library of Congress Cataloging-in-Publication Data
Duchesne, Christiane, 1949-
Peter's secret / by Christiane Duchesne ; illustrated by Mylene Pratt.
p. cm. — (Read-it! readers)
Summary: Peter has not told anyone the secret of why he is different from other
children, but when a new student joins his class, he wonders if he can tell her.
ISBN 1-4048-1351-9 (hard cover)
[1. Secrets—Fiction. 2. Friendship—Fiction. 3. People with disabilities—Fiction.]
I. Pratt, Mylène, ill. II. Title. III. Series.

PZ7.D8568Pe 2005
[E]—dc22
2005003897

Peter's Secret

by Christiane Duchesne
illustrated by Myléne Pratt

Special thanks to our advisers for their expertise:

Adria F. Klein, Ph.D.
Professor Emeritus, California State University
San Bernardino, California

Susan Kesselring, M.A.
Literacy Educator
Rosemount–Apple Valley–Eagan (Minnesota) School District

PiCTURE WiNDOW BOOKS
Minneapolis, Minnesota

On the way to school, among
the tall pines and birch trees,
Peter walked along, looking
at his feet.

"Left, right, left, right …
and left again. Left,
left, left!" he sang.

With his right foot in
his right hand, Peter
hopped along on one leg.

"Left, left, left, left …" he said.

A root was sticking out next to a hole.

"If I was like everybody else, I would have
fallen in the hole," said Peter.

Peter wasn't like other children. But they didn't know that. He kept that secret safe.

Peter was smaller than other children. He didn't jump as high. He never ran. He didn't know how to swim or play ball.

But he owned a little black horse
named Nero.

Nobody else at school had a horse.
Peter wasn't like the other children.

At school, a girl came into the classroom. She had hair as black as Nero's mane. She said she came from another school. She said she'd just changed houses, changed schools, and changed friends.

She smiled and looked right at Peter. She said her name was Lola.

Everyone was running, laughing, and
yelling. Everyone was leaving school.
The day was over!

Peter slowly began walking home. He
turned around and saw Lola, her braid
bouncing in the air.

"Which way are you going home?"
asked Lola.

"That way," answered Peter, pointing
toward the road with the tall pines.

"Then I'll go that way, too," said Lola
with a smile.

13

On the road with the tall pines, Lola started running.

"No!" yelled Peter. "Don't run!"

Lola wanted to run to the first birch tree. She started to gallop, with her braid bouncing on her back.

"The first one there gets a prize!" she yelled.

Out of breath and smiling, she leaned
against the birch tree and watched Peter.

Peter caught up to Lola at the first birch.

"I'm going to run to the pine tree that lost
its head. Over there, do you see it?"
she asked.

17

"Lola, don't run," Peter begged.

Lola wondered. Is he lazy? Do his feet hurt? Who is this funny kid who doesn't want to run?

Lola and Peter slowly walked toward the big pine that had lost its head.

"Near my house, the trees lost their heads, too. Crack! The ice snapped them off. But I didn't lose mine," she laughed.

Lola talked about the forest near her old house. It was as beautiful as this one.

Peter wondered if he should tell her his secret. Could he trust her?

He decided he could trust her.

"Lola, I can't run with you. I don't have any muscles in my legs," Peter said.

Without muscles, Peter's legs didn't have any spark. His legs were cold and tired.

"My legs are going to get well, but it will take a long time. I have to build up the muscles," Peter said.

"Then I'll walk with you until you can run with me," said Lola.

They slowly walked toward his house.

"That's where I live," he said, showing her the vast golden field and the house far in the distance.

25

Just then, Nero came up, proud and prancing, with deep, dark eyes.

"That's my horse!" Peter said.

Then, he grabbed Nero's thick mane and climbed onto his back.

"Climb up, Lola. I can't run," said Peter, "but Nero can run for me."

Peter helped Lola onto the horse's back.

Lola closed her eyes, and
they galloped until they felt
like they were flying.

If Nero could have smiled,
he would have. He had
never seen Peter this
happy before.

"Lola, please don't tell anyone about my legs. This is a secret just between us, OK?" Peter said.

"I won't tell anyone your secret," she promised.

Nero galloped even faster. He decided to take them to the far end of the field, where the sun would soon set.

More *Read-it!* Readers

Bright pictures and fun stories help you practice your reading skills. Look for more books at your level.

Alex and Sarah by Gilles Tibo
Alex and the Team Jersey by Gilles Tibo
Alex and Toolie by Gilles Tibo
Clever Cat by Karen Wallace
Flora McQuack by Penny Dolan
Izzie's Idea by Jillian Powell
Mysteries for Felicio by Mireille Villeneuve
Naughty Nancy by Anne Cassidy
Parents Do the Weirdest Things! by Louise Tondreau-Levert
Peppy, Patch, and the Bath by Marisol Sarrazin
Peppy, Patch, and the Postman by Marisol Sarrazin
Peppy, Patch, and the Socks by Marisol Sarrazin
Peter's Secret by Christiane Duchesne
The Princess and the Frog by Margaret Nash
Rumble Meets Shelby Spider by Felicia Law
Rumble the Dragon's Cave by Felicia Law
Run! by Sue Ferraby
Sausages! by Anne Adeney
Theodore the Millipede by Carole Tremblay
The Truth About Hansel and Gretel by Karina Law
Willie the Whale by Joy Oades

Looking for a specific title or level? A complete list of *Read-it!* Readers is available on our Web site:
www.picturewindowbooks.com